Raggedy Ann's
Words of Friendship

Other Titles in the Raggedy Ann Collection:

Raggedy Ann's
Words of Friendship

Kind Thoughts for One and All

from the works of Johnny Gruelle

SIMON & SCHUSTER BOOKS FOR YOUNG READERS

New York   London   Toronto   Sydney   Singapore

Let us start a garden, you and I.
Let us turn the soil of acquaintanceship
And in this fertile ground plant kindly thoughts;
Let us pull all weeds of envy and selfishness
And destroy them!

Let us water our garden with the dew of sympathy.
Let us keep our growing plants in the sunshine of love
And happiness is ours; our garden is filled
With the beautiful flowers of friendship.

Friendship—
"is doing unselfish deeds and
kindly acts for those in need."

Friendship—

"is just like a great, great, big music box which old Mister Sun winds up every night before he goes to bed, so that it will start bright and early in the morning, playing and sending out happy sounds for everyone's pleasure."

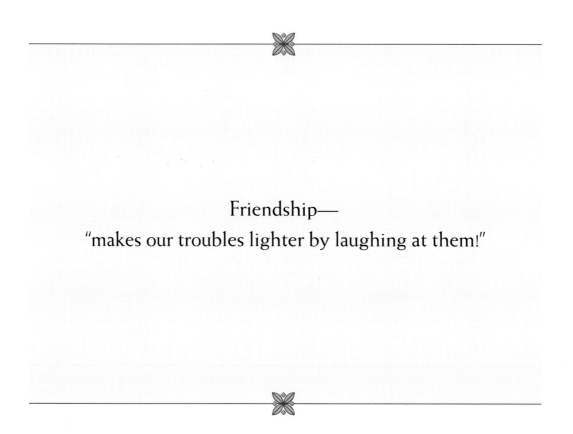

Friendship—

"makes our troubles lighter by laughing at them!"

Friendship—
"is when someone gives us a moment of happiness . . .
and we reflect that happiness from our sunny
hearts to someone else, and so in turn it is
reflected to others, on and on!"

Friendship—
"is being generous and unselfish,
even to those who are unkind to us."

Friendship—
"means . . . in helping others we gain love and
friendship and add to the sunniness in our own hearts."

Friendship—
"is a whole lot more fun than
being gruff or grumpy!"

Friendship—
"means if we search for gladness along
the path of our journeys . . . it measures
out into a long sunshiny adventure."

Friendship—
"is being kind and unselfish,
then those who meet us will be filled
with good thoughts and love for us!"

Friendship—

"means whenever you do something kindly for
another, you plant a seed inside your own heart,
which grows into a happiness blossom, and,
for every speck of fun you give another,
you receive an echo of that fun yourself!"

Friendship—
"gives your heart a 'sunshine bath' by saying,
'I love everyone!'"

J. GRUELLE

Friendship—
"means unhappiness can never creep in
when our hearts are filled with the
sunshine of unselfish love."

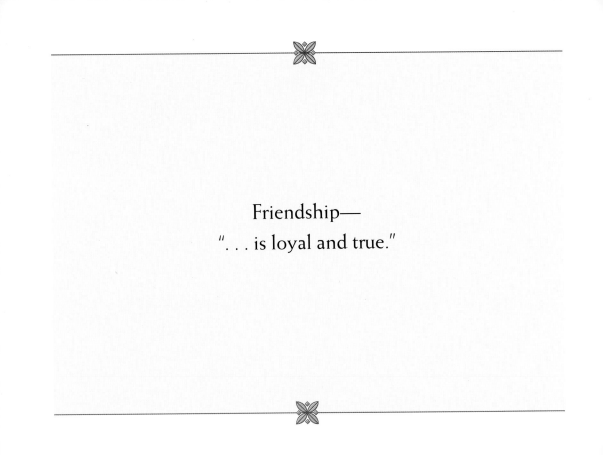

Friendship—

". . . is loyal and true."

Friendship—
"shines right through even the
shabbiest of clothes."

Friendship—
"is the pleasure of having wished
good things for our friends!"

Friendship—

"means kindly friends who love us!"

"And, as you surely must know, there is no feeling which brings as much true sunshine to our hearts as the happiness of an honest, loving friendship."

SIMON & SCHUSTER BOOKS FOR YOUNG READERS
An imprint of Simon & Schuster Children's Publishing Division
1230 Avenue of the Americas, New York, New York 10020

Library of Congress Cataloging-in-Publication Data
Gruelle, Johnny, 1880–1938.
Raggedy Ann's words of friendship: kind thoughts for one and all / from the works of Johnny Gruelle.
p. cm.
ISBN 0-689-84638-X
1. Friendship—Juvenile literature. [1. Friendship.]
BJ1533.F8 G78 2002
177'.62—dc21   2001020778